SHARK GIRL AND BELLY BUTTON

written and illustrated by
Casey Riordan Millard

blue manatee press | Cincinnati, OH

Published by blue manatee press,
Cincinnati, Ohio.
blue manatee press and associated logo
are registered trademarks of Arete Ventures, LLC.

First Edition: Fall, 2014.

Library of Congress Cataloging-In-Publication Data
Millard, Casey R.
Shark Girl and Belly Button / by Casey Riordan Millard—1st ed.
Summary: Shark Girl sees the world in a worried way, while her best friend,
Belly Button, has a more positive outlook.
Together they have five trifles—writing a letter, making paper dolls, going to a party, visiting
the playground, and appreciating the value of things, especially one's friends.
These simple stories combine humor, emotion, and insight, inviting readers to look beyond
physical appearance into the thoughts and dreams we all share.

ISBN-13 (hardcover): 978-1936669196
[Juvenile Fiction - Family/Parents. 2. Juvenile Fiction – New Experience.]
Printed in the USA.

Artwork was created with watercolor, gouache, and Princeton Select brushes on
Fabriano Artistico 300 lb hot press watercolor paper.

Editorial Design by Mayte Suarez.

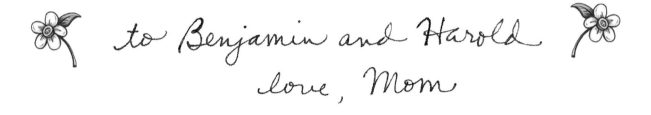

to Benjamin and Harold
love, Mom

FIVE TRIFLES

1. Thank You Note

2. Paper Dolls

3. The Party

4. Playground

5. Free

A trifle is something
of little importance.

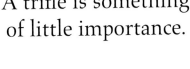

Or it's a giant,
fluffy cake!

Dear Aunt Lorraine…

Isn't she just a friend
of the family?

An unofficial "Aunt?"

...The picture frame you sent
me is very nice...

But to send you something
"just because."

She must really care about you.

...I am going to save it in the
tissue until I see you again,
so we can take our picture
together to go inside...

Doesn't she live overseas?

...Then I will always
remember our special
time together...

I thought she was afraid of flying?

...Most sincere love,
your niece.

You know, you never actually said,
"*thank you?*"

P.S. Thank you a
hundred, million,
billion times.

Perfect.

PAPER DOLLS

I got this book of paper dolls.

They look old-fashioned.

They're Victorian.
I wish I had dresses like these.

Tiny paper dresses are
the next best thing.

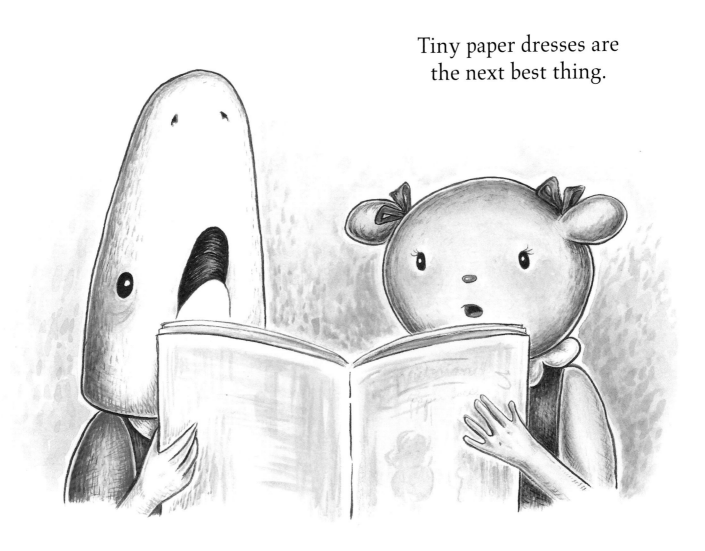

Look how pretty her hair is.
It's drawn really well.

Don't you wish you could draw
your hair on every day?

She has *dozens* of outfits.
Playtime.
School time.
Fancy...

Who knew Victorian girls
were so active?

Which one are you going
to cut out first?

Oh, I'm not cutting
them out.
That would wreck
the book!

But she'll never get to wear
her ice skating outfit.

She's wearing it right now
in my head.

I guess that will have to
be enough.

It is.
I know she's okay with it.

PLAYGROUND

Why so glum?

Vicki won't play with me today.

She's over there with Ronnie.

Ronnie got this high-bounce
ball that goes *really* high.

It's not even Ronnie's ball- she
didn't buy it, she found it!

You should be happy for Ronnie
that she found such a great toy.
What a lucky duck.

I never find anything.

You should ask to play with them.
I'm sure you could all have fun together.

I don't think so.

Vicki will get over the ball.
You'll see.

No way.
Our friendship is over.

I've got to get rid of that ball.

Let's think about this
for a minute.

Oh, boy. Here we go.

I've got a plan.

THE PARTY

Are you sure this
is the right house?

Pretty sure.

It says right here on the invitation-
323 Flora Lane. One o'clock.

Then where is everybody?

Maybe it's a surprise party for me,
and they are all hiding!

It's Vicki's birthday party.
I brought her a smelly candle.

I hope nothing bad happened.

What if there was some kind
of emergency and everyone
had to evacuate?

What if Vicki regrets inviting me and
changed the location of the party?

What did I do to make her angry?

WHAT A WASTE OF A
SUNDAY AFTERNOON!

It's Saturday.

Really?

Yep.

This feels right.

I liked my dress better
yesterday though.

You look lovely.

FREE

Whoa. Where'd you get her?

She was free.

Lucky!

You should name her Penny.

Because she is lucky?

Because nothing is really free.

Oh. Heavy.

She sort of has a funny eye.

No she doesn't.
She can't help it.

I don't like the way she is looking at me.

Penny is sweet.

She's creeping me out. I'm going home.

Well, OK. Good night.